ELLIOTT CARTER

BRASS QUINTET

(1974)

1993 edition

AMP-7521

Associated Music Publishers, Inc.

DISTRIBUTED BY

HAL•LEONARD®

7777 W. BLUEMOUND RD. P.O. BOX 13819 MILWAUKEE, WI 53213

PROGRAM NOTES

The Brass Quintet was written during the summer of 1974 for the American Brass Quintet which commissioned the work. This group gave its première on October 20, 1974 at a Charles Ives Festival broadcast by the BBC from London, and its American première at the Library of Congress on November 15, 1974, and has recorded the work for Columbia Records.

The music, being almost constantly multilayered, as is my *Second String Quartet,* separates the players by individualizing their parts, but not completely, because each instrument shares parts of its repertory with one of the others. The first trumpet, for instance, near the beginning plays in a trio with the second trumpet and tenor trombone featuring the minor sixth in light, irregular chords of which the character and interval become part of the repertory of the three participating instruments. A bit later, the first trumpet plays another trio with the horn and bass trombone that features fanfares and quiet, majestic music based on the perfect fifth, which then become part of the repertory of these three instruments. The horn, which has the largest repertory of all, however also frequently uses the augmented fourth which it does not share with any of the others.

All of the contrasting characters and their related musical intervals form a multilayered piece planned along the following pattern: Every third (that is, the first, fourth, seventh etc.) of its overlapping 19 short sections is a brief five-part quodlibet in which the instruments oppose each other with contrasting parts of their individual repertories. Between these is a duo preceded or followed by a trio in which two or three instruments join in music of similar character. Each duo and trio has a different instrumentation.

The general plan is interrupted midway through the work by a relatively extended unaccompanied horn solo which is cut off by angry octaves from the others. The slow music which began the piece and forms the background of the first three quodlibets is abandoned after the last of these, only to return in extended form near the end. The entire work, in fact, can be heard as one long, slow movement with interruptions.

This quintet, rather than employing all the resources of color possible with modern mutes for the brass, relies primarily on linear material, textures and the instrumental virtuosity for which the American Brass Quintet is notable.

E.C.

FORMAL PLAN

Measures

1- 12: *Quodlibet:* preliminary statement of the "calm" slow movement, interrupted in m.5-7 by the horn and followed by a brief outburst by all the instruments, each contributing a different fragment of its own part.

13- 37: *Trio for two trumpets and trombone 1:* "lightly", featuring the minor sixth.

30- 48: *Duo for trombone 2 accompanied by the horn:* "vigorous", featuring the perfect fourth.

48- 71: *Quodlibet:* centered around the "angry" recitative of trombone 1, combined at times with trombone 2 and horn, prefiguring their trio after 284, while trumpet 1 plays its "flowing" music and the others continue the "calm" music that does not stop until m.142.

72-100: *Duo for trumpet 2 and horn, both muted*: "humorous", featuring the minor third.

93-118: *Trio for trumpet 1, horn and trombone 2*: "majestic", featuring the perfect fifth in chords and fanfares.

116-132: *Quodlibet*: combines the "humorous", "majestic" and "calm" movements with a solo of trombone 1 that prefigures its 'dramatic' solo after m.387.

133-158: *Trio for two trumpets and horn*: "smoothly flowing", featuring the major second.

150-178: *Duo for two trombones*: "extravagant", featuring the major third in glissandos and "rips".

169-201: *Quodlibet*: while the trombone duo continues, the "majestic" and "humorous" movements are recalled. After a brief reference to the outburst in the first quodlibet the section ends with a continuation of the "humorous" music by trumpet 2 and horn that ends at m.210.

201-235: *Trio for trumpet 1 accompanied by two trombones*: "lyric", featuring the major sixth.

220-258: *Horn solo*: "menacing", features the augmented fourth and the other intervals in the horn's repertory.

249-269: *Quodlibet*: the others interject while the horn continues.

261-295: *Duo for two trumpets*: "furious", features the major seventh.

284-316: *Trio for horn and two trombones*: "angry", features the minor second and minor ninth.

306-341: *Quodlibet*: during m.306-314, trumpet 1 speeds up and trumpet 2 slows down, each recalling a different fragment of their own part, as the other three finish their trio. Then there is a violent outburst to which each player contributes in his own way.

338-389: *slow movement*: "calm".

387-395: *Duo for trombone 1 accompanied by trumpet 2, muted*: "dramatic", featuring the minor seventh.

396-400: *Coda*: during the many trills, previous moments are recalled: 397, the trombone duo of m.150; 398, the trumpet duo at 261; 398, horn at 257; 399, the trio at m.13.

E.C.

For the American Brass Quintet

BRASS QUINTET

(Transposed Score)

ELLIOTT CARTER
(1974)

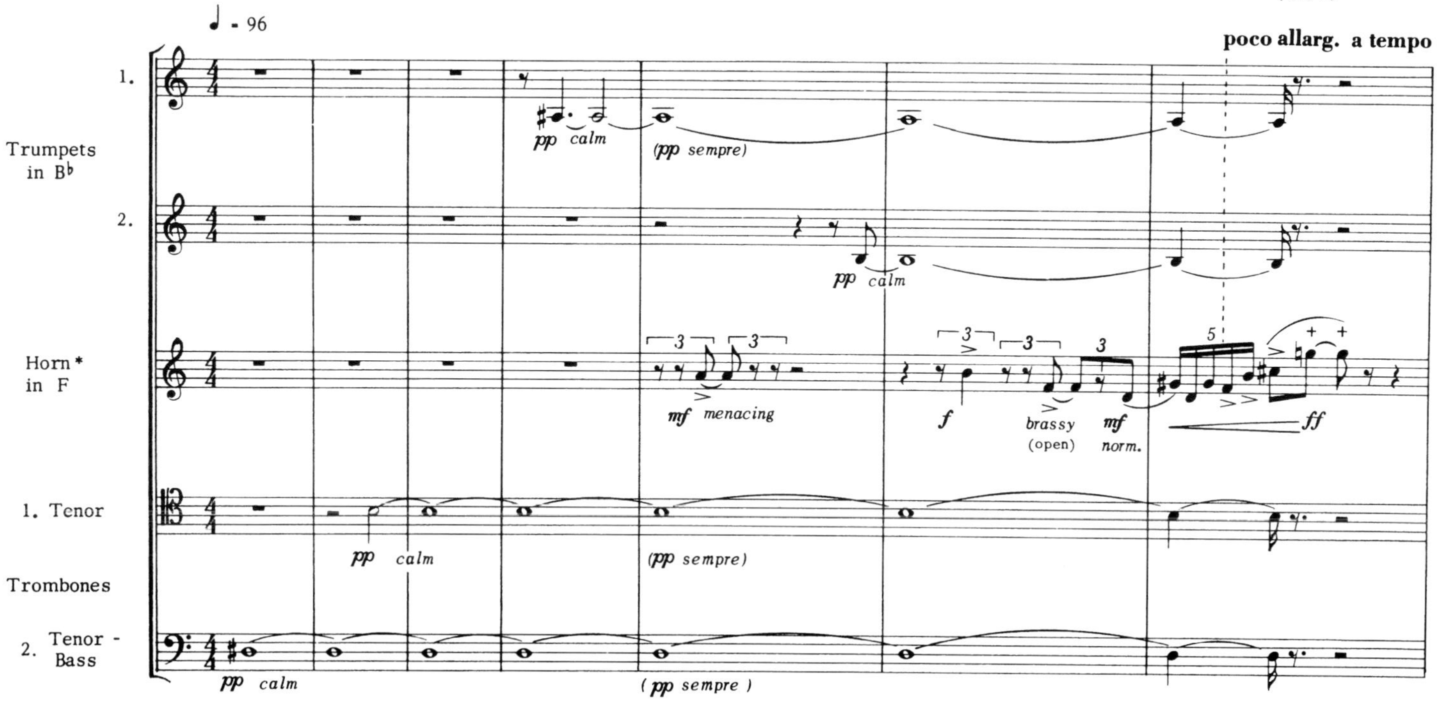

*The horn is notated one fifth above actual sound, regardless of clef.
Trombones, m. 11, etc.: All "rips" should sound as many notes as possible.

Dynamics: The dynamic markings of this score are "absolute" - that is, forte in the horn part should sound as loud as the forte of the other players, etc.

12
(♩ = 96)
lightly
lightly
lightly
pp sempre
calm
pp calm
16
(pp sempre)
mf espr.
mf espr.
(pp sempre)
21
p sub.
p sub.
p sub.
(pp sempre)

26
30
(𝅗𝅥 =48)
vigorous
to the fore
vigorous
34
to the fore
più f

38
♩. = 60
(string. [optional] as fast as possible)
(♩. = 60)
f marc.
41
(♩ = 90 or faster)
pp calm
43
(pp sempre)

46
(ritardando
= 45)
(pp)
(pp)
(pp sempre)
f
più f
meno f
ff
p
(cresc.)
pp
ff angry
menof
p sub.
pp calm
49
(♩. = 60)
mf flowing
p
ff angry
pp calm
53
(pp sempre)

* For measures 72-95 and 194-210, the horn player should use a mute that matches as nearly as possible the nasal quality of that of the second trumpet.

74
marc.
mf sub.
(pp sempre)
78
82
Tpt. 2
Horn
86
(♪. = 144)

90
(♪. = 144)
♩ = 72
majestic
calm
majestic
94
97
(♩. = 48)
secco
sim.
senza sord.
espr.
majestic
secco
secco
sim.

100
= 96
103
Tpt. 1
Horn
Tbn. 2
meno f
108
= 96
senza sord.
pp calm

112
(♪. = 96)
← ♪ → (♩ = 72)
f
mp - p
mp - p
mp - p
mp - p
mp - p
(pp)
f espr.
mf
pp calm
mf
mp - p
mp - p
mp - p
mp - p
pp calm
Solo
mf
mp
cant. espr., legato
mf
f
mp - p
mp - p
mp - p
mp - p
mp - p
117
mp - p
p
p
mp
p
mp
p
(pp)
pp espr.
p
mf
humorous
mp
p
mf
(Solo)
mp
mf
mf
pp calm
121
← ♩ = ♩. →
pp
p
p
p
p
mp
mf
pp calm
pp calm
mf
legato sempre
meno f
(pp)
p
vigorous
mf

125
♩ = ♩. ♩. = 72
pp calm
(pp)
(pp)
meno f
(pp sempre)
meno f
mp
mf
p
p
(p)
mp
mf
f
128
♪ (𝅗𝅥 = 54)
♩ = ♩. ♩. = 54
(pp)
p espr.
mf
p
pp calm
p
(pp)
(pp)
p
f (non dim.)
mf
f
pp calm
(pp)
p
132
pp
pp smoothly flowing
pp
p
p smoothly flowing
pp
p
pp
pp smoothly flowing
p
pp calm
pp

135
(♩ = 81)
(♩. = 54)
marc.
calm
138
♩. = 72
marc.
calm
141
♩ = 90
marc.
marc.

144
Tpt. 1
Tpt. 2
Horn
♩ = 52.5 (♩ = 105)
146
148
(♩. = 70)
150
(♩ = 52.5, ♩ = 105)
mf extravagant
"rip"
gliss.
extravagant

152
(♩ = 105)
marc.
marc.
154
155

157
♩ = 84
extravagant
159
(♪. = 112)
Tbn. 1
Tbn. 2
espr.
p sub.
162
♩ = 112
cresc. poco a poco
cresc. poco a poco
164
"rip"
166
gliss.
"rip"
molto espr.
molto espr.

✲ "rip"-s notated by a connecting line are to be played in the same way as those previously notated in detail.

* From m. 183 through 192: Tpt.1, not muted, should be evenly balanced with Tpt.2, muted.

191
(♩ = 96)
espr.
humorous
angry
194
(♪ = 128)
con sord.
humorous
197

200
♪ =106.7 (♩. = 53.3)
to the fore
mf (cantabile)
lyric
accomp.
accomp.
p espr.
lyric
202
♩ = 80
Tpt.2 : alternate notation
Horn: alternate notation
lyric

204
(♩=80)
[Tpt.2: alternate notation]
[Horn: alternate notation]
p 3 espr., legato
p espr., legato
206
mf espr.

208
meno f
f - mf
mf - p
p sub.
210
fp

213
(♩= 80)
Tpt. 1
Tbn. 1
Tbn. 2
216
220
senza sord.
menacing
flt.
gliss.
pp sub.
marc.
più f
224

*Trill on one note: fingerings for the G and F double sharp should be used that produce the same pitch but with two different colorations.

⌖ "Echo - tone": This special effect is produced by fingering the pitch a semitone higher than the written note and flatting it by cupping the hand in the bell - sometimes called half - stopping. It is described in Gunther Schuller's Horn Technique, Oxford university Press and in Domenico Ceccarossi's Le Possibilità Coloristiche del Corno. (Rome, 1949) It is indicated by the sign: ⌖

249
(♩=100)
angry
f (non dim.)
(echo tone)
pp dolce
253
𝅗𝅥 = 60
257
marc.
𝅘𝅥𝅮. = 96

260
(♩=72, ♪. = 96)
furious
marc.
ff sub.
f sub.
mf sub.
p sub.
più f
f-p
263
mf-p
266
mp
mf-p

269
(♩ = 72)
272
Tpt. 1
Tpt. 2
(𝅗𝅥 = 54, ♩ = 108)
276
278
rubato
a tempo
281
(𝅗𝅥 = 54)
marc.
sub.

284
♩ = 90
angry
angry
angry
286
(♩. = 60)
mf sub.
♩ =60, ♩ = 120
mp mf sub.
289
mf sub.
sub.
ff sub. f
f sub.
f sub.
ff sub.
f sub.

292
(𝅗𝅥 = 60)
295
299
Horn
Tbn. 1
Tbn. 2
[optional]
(hurry slightly - - - - a tempo)
302
Horn
Tbn. 1
Tbn. 2
[optional]
(hurry slightly - - - - a tempo)

306
(senza sord.)
con sord.
humorous
sempre quasi accel.
sempre quasi rit.
309
(mf sempre)
313
agitated
più f

318
♩ = 60
accel.
♩ = 126
cresc. poco a poco
dramatic
humorous
gliss.
angry
senza sord.
321
326
(♩. = 84)
♩ = 84

331
marcatiss.
335
poco meno f
molto
𝅗𝅥 = 56
338
calm
sub.
dramatic
espr.

342
(𝅗𝅥 = 56)
p espr.
mf
p
ppp
pp calm
p espr
347
pp
calm
352
mp
mf
(p)

357
ten.
362
367

371 (𝅗𝅥 = 56)
376
380

* Tpt. 2, mm. 387 - 391 : The fast figures are played rubato; the general tempo should not change.

May 15 - August 29,1974
Aspen-Waccabuc

Trumpet 1 in B♭

ELLIOTT CARTER

BRASS QUINTET

(1974)

1993 edition

Associated Music Publishers, Inc.

DISTRIBUTED BY
HAL•LEONARD®
7777 W. BLUEMOUND RD. P.O. BOX 13819 MILWAUKEE, WI 53213

B♭ Trumpet 1

For the American Brass Quintet

BRASS QUINTET

ELLIOTT CARTER
(1974)

Dynamics: The dynamic markings are "absolute" - that is, forte in one part should sound as loud as the forte of the other players.

38
♩. = 60 (string. [optional] - - - as fast as possible)
Tbn.2
41
Tbn.2
(♩= 90 or faster)
pp calm
44
(ritardando
(pp sempre)
47
♩= 45)
Hn.
Tbn.1
(♩. = 60)
mf
flowing
p
51
p
pp
55
pp
pp
pp
(pp)
60
(pp)
(♩ = 90)

B♭ Trumpet 1

(♩ =90)
Tbn.2
Tbn.1
pp calm
♩ = 108
Tpt.2
Hn.
(pp sempre)
Tpt.2
(♪. =144)
Tpt.2
♩ = 72
p majestic
p secco
(♩. = 48)
sim.
♩ =96
(pp)
♪. = 96

114
119
122
126
133
136
139
Tpt.2
Hn.
Tbn. 1
calm
smoothly flowing
(♩ = 72)
♩. = 72
(𝅗𝅥 = 54)
♩. = 54
(♩ = 81)
(♩. = 54)

B♭ Trumpet 1

142
♩ = 90
Tpt.2
(Hn.)
145
♩ = 52.5 (♩ = 105)
Hn.
Tpt.2
147
Hn.
(♩. = 70)
Tpt.2
149
(♩ = 52.5, ♩ = 105)
Tpt.2
Hn.
151
Tpt.2
Hn.
Hn.

153
Tpt.2
154
155
Hn.
Tpt.2
156
157
♩ = 84
159
(♪ = 112)
♩ = 112
167
Tbn.1
"rip"
molto espr.

B♭ Trumpet 1

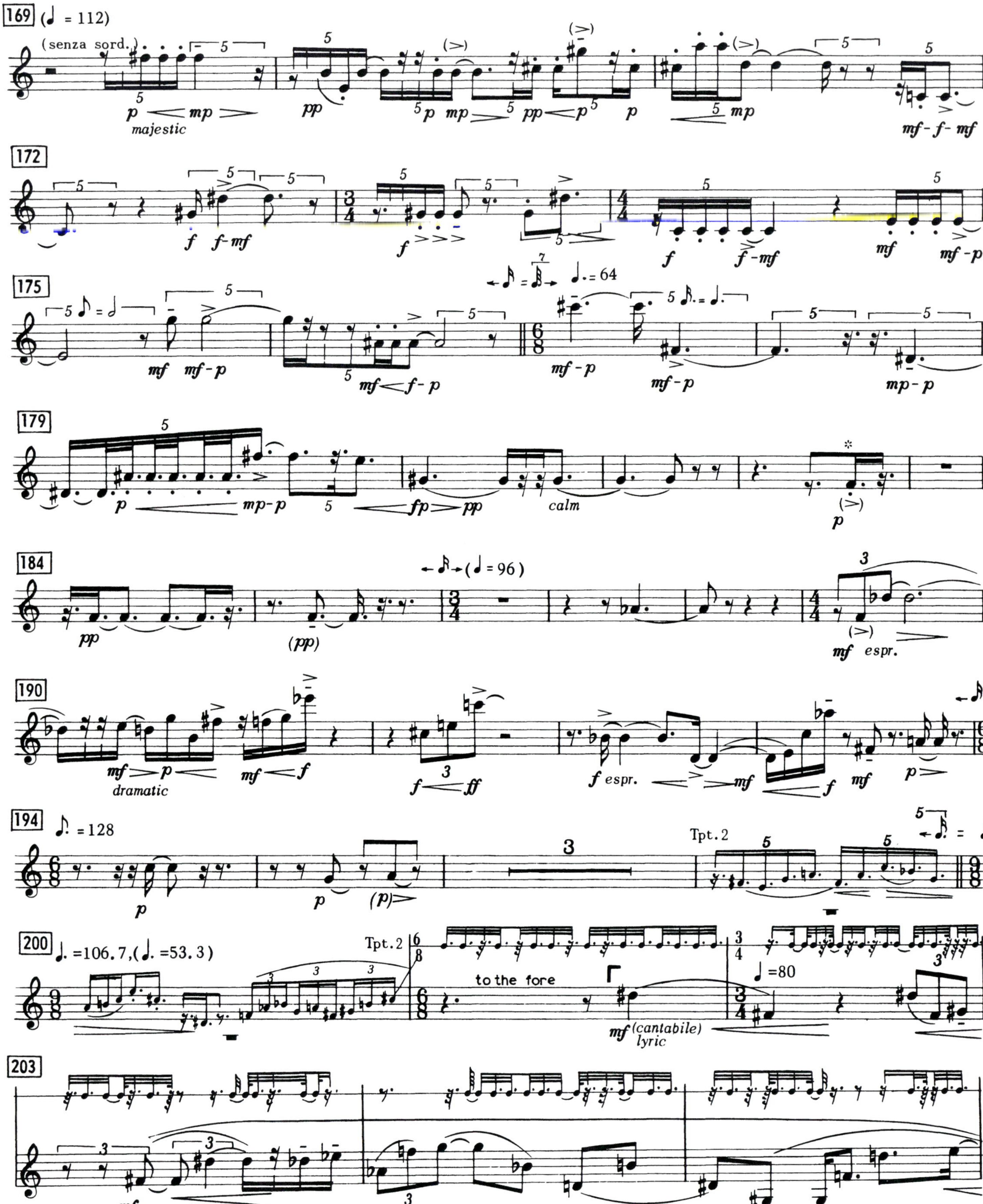

✲ m. 182-192, Tpt. 1 not muted, should be evenly balanced with Tpt. 2 , muted

206
209
Tbn. 1
Tbr. 2
meno f
f - mf
212
216
più f
220
224
228
ff molto espr.
232
♩ = 100
f - mf
f - p

string. rit.
a tempo
accel.
tempo
Rubato (accel.)
broaden a little
Hn.
a tempo
broaden
in tempo
angry
(non dim.)
Tbn.1
Tbn.2
Hn.
Tpt.2
furious
marc.

B♭ Trumpet 1

276
Tpt. 2
279
rubato
a tempo
282
marc.
284
♩ = 90
(♩. = 60)
287
𝅗𝅥 = 60, ♩ = 120
290
293

B♭ Trumpet 1

301
(hurry - a tempo)
[optional]
(hurry slightly - - - a tempo)
Hn.
Tbn. 1
Tbn. 2
Tpt. 2
307
(senza sord.)
f sempre quasi accel.
310
(mf sempre)
314
f agitated
318
accel.
cresc. poco a poco
dramatic
322
dramatic
327
332
ff marcatiss.
336
poco meno
molto
p calm

B♭ Trumpet 1

339
f sub.
dramatic
(f)
p calm
pp
p espr.
3
mf
p
344
ppp
pp calm
pp
p
350
ppp
357
mp
mf
362
(pp)
367
372
f
377
382
386
387
= 70
poco accel.
poco rit.
2
Tpt. 2
(poco rit.)
7
395
= 40 (= 80)
ff marc.
dramatic
398
ff
fff

B♭ Trumpet 2

For the American Brass Quintet

BRASS QUINTET

ELLIOTT CARTER
(1974)

Dynamics: The dynamic markings are "absolute" - that is, forte in one part should sound as loud as the forte of the other players.

B♭ Trumpet 2

42
(♩ =90 or faster)
Tb.2
pp calm
45
(ritardando
=45)
(pp sempre)
48
(♩. =60)
Tb.2
Tb.1
53
(pp sempre)
59
Tb.2
Tpt.1
(♩ = 90)
(pp sempre)
65
Tpt. 1

B♭ Trumpet 2

♩ = 108
72
Hn.
con sord.
mf
humorous
mp
mf
p
mp
p
mf
f
marc.
mf sub.
76
mp
mf
mf
mf
(mf)
p
f
80
5
f
mf
p
mf
mf - p
83
f - mf
f
f
mf
p
86
mf
p
(♪. = 144)
12
16
mp
mf
mp
f
89
(f)
mf
mp
mf
9
16
mp
mf
♩ = 72
92
ff
mf
f
mf
p
mf
95
f
p
mf
mf
♩. = 48
6
8
mp
mf
98
f
mf
mp
p
100
♩ = 96
(p)
7

108
(♩= 96)
Tpt.1
Hn.
Tb.2
Tpt.1
senza sord.
pp calm
♩. =96
113
(♩ =72)
f espr.
mf
pp calm
118
pp espr.
p
mp
122
Tpt.1
Tb.1
mf
pp calm
♩. = 72
126
(𝅗𝅥 = 54)
p espr.
mf
p
pp calm
130
♩. = 54
Tpt.1
Tba.1
Tpt.1
p
p smoothly flowing
pp

B♭ Trumpet 2

Tpt. 1
= 81
= 54
Tpt. 1
= 72
Hn.
= 90
= 52.5 (= 105)
= 70
Tpt. 1
(= 52.5, = 105)
Hn.
Tpt. 1
= 84
(= 112)
= 112

B♭ Trumpet 2

* m. 182-192, Tpt. 1 not muted, should be evenly balanced with Tpt. 2, muted

B♭ Trumpet 2

198
Tbn. 2
Hn.
♪. = 106.7 (♩. = 53.3)
201
Tpt. 2 alternate notation
♩ = 80
accomp.
203
205
207
209

B♭ Trumpet 2

211 (♩= 80)
220
Tpt.1
senza sord.
225
Tpt.1
232
♩ = 100
238
string. rit.
a tempo
accel. a tempo
Rubato (accel.) . . .
247
Hn.
a tempo
broaden
a tempo
(♩ = 100)
(non dim.)
angry
251
𝅗𝅥 =60
256
marc.
259
♩. = 96
Tpt.1
Tbn.1+2
Hn.
Tbn.1
Tbn.2
(♩ =72, ♪. =96)
furious
marc.
262
sub.
265
sub.

B♭ Trumpet 2

B♭ Trumpet 2

301
(𝅗𝅥 = 60)
(hurry a tempo)
2
Hn.
[optional]
(hurry slightly - - - - - - a tempo)
Tbn. 1
306
Hn.
Tbn. 2
con sord.
f
humorous
Tpt. 1
sempre quasi rit.
308
Tpt. 1
mf
f
mf
311
più f
314
f
mf
f
mf
318
♩ = 60
accel.
f
♩ = 126
f
humorous
321
senza sord.
f
mf
f
p
mp
f
fp
mf
dramatic

B♭ Trumpet 2

325
♩. = 84
♪ = ♪
ff
ff
♩ = 84
♩. = ♩
f
mf
f
mf
f
fp
mp
330
3
mf
f
ff
f
mf
f
ff
334
sff
ff marcatiss.
poco meno f
molto
♩. = 𝅗𝅥
337
𝅗𝅥 = 56
fff
ff
9
f
9
f
9
p calm
340
pp
p
pp
p espr.
mf
p
ppp
345
3
Tpt. 1
Hn.
pp calm
352
ppp
pp

B♭ Trumpet 2

* mm. 387 - 394: The fast figures are played rubato; the general tempo should not change.

Trombone 1

For the American Brass Quintet

BRASS QUINTET

ELLIOTT CARTER
(1974)

All "rips" should sound as many notes as possible.

Dynamics: The dynamic markings are "absolute" - that is, forte in one part should sound as loud as the forte of the other players.

Trombone 1

40
Tbn.2 - - - - - as fast as possible)
42
(♩ = 90 or faster)
Tbn.2
pp calm
45
(ritardando - - - - - - - 𝅗𝅥 = 45)
pp
48
Hn.
(♩. = 60)
ff angry
f
ff
Tpt.1
52
Tpt.1
f
f
56
Tb.2
f
f
ff
pp calm

Trombone 1

61
Tpt.1
(♩= 90)
Tbn.2
mf
f
ff
angry
67
Tpt.1
♩= 108
Tpt.2
pp calm
(pp sempre)
74
Tpt.2
80
2
4
(♪. = 144)
3
Tbn.2
♩= 72
91
Tpt.2
ff
pp calm
♩=96
Tpt.2
97
♩. =48
9

Trombone 1

(♩. = 96)
110
Tpt.1
pp calm
115
(♩ = 72)
Solo
mf
mp
cant. espr., legato
mf
(Solo)
mp
120
125
mf
legato sempre
meno f
♩. = 72
meno f
meno f
128
(𝅗𝅥 = 54)
others
f (non dim.)
mf
f
Tpt.1
♩. = 54
pp calm
Tpt.2
133
♩ =81
Tpt.1
Hn.
Tpt.2
(♩. = 54)
138
Hn.
Tpt.1
♩. = 72
♩ = 90
Tbn.2
mf
mf-p
pp calm
mp
143
Tbn.2
mf
marc.
𝅗𝅥 = 52.5
♩. = 70
Tpt.2
Hn.
150
(𝅗𝅥 = 52.5, ♩ = 105)
Hn.
Tbn.2
VI
IV
III
V
II
"rip"
mf extravagant
f
mf
f
mf

152
Tpt.1
Tbn.2
mf
f
mp
marc.
Hn.
155
Tpt.1
mf-p
extravagant
158
♩ = 84
(♪. = 112)
espr.
161
♩ = 112
cresc. poco a poco
164
"rip"
166
gliss.
ff
molto espr.
169
legato
sff
"rip"
(as before)
173
ff
177
♩. = 64
pp
p espr.
angry
sff-p

Trombone 1

184
(♩. =64)
p espr.
♪ ♩ = 96
pp
Hn.
Tbn. 2
mf espr.
mf
190
p
dramatic
f
ff
sf - mf
angry
ff
mf
193
Trp. 2
Trp.1
Hn.
Trp.1
♪. = 128
Tbn. 2
Trp.1
Trb. 2
f
mf
p
mf
p
p
(p)
Hn.
196
Tpt. 2
Hn.
Tbn. 2
Trp. 2
(4)
p
(p)
mf
mp
p
Tbn. 2
199
Tpt. 2
♪. = 106.7 (♩. = 53.3)
Tpt. 1
♩ = 80
Hn.
mf
p
lyric
mf
203
p
p
pp
p espr., legato
206
mf
p
mf
mf - p

209
mp
mf-p
fp
mf
f
mp
213
f
3
mf
mp
p
217
220
224
fp
227
ff
ff-f
231
ff-mf
ff-
Hn.
♩ = 100
234
2

Trombone 1

238
string.
rit.
a tempo
accel.
a tempo
Rubato (accel.)
247
Hn.
broaden a little
atempo
broaden
in tempo
f (non dim.)
angry
250
256
259
Tpt. 1
Hn.
Tbn. 2
262
Tpt. 2
265
268
275
rubato
a tempo

283
angry
285
♩ = 90
♩. = 60
288
𝅗𝅥 = 60, ♩ = 120
f sub.
292
f sub.
297
300
304
308
312
315
Tpt. 1
♩ =60
accel.

Trombone 1

319
♩ = 126
mf
dramatic
f
angry
323
p
mp
fp
dramatic
ff
♪ ♩. = 84
fp
327
♩ = 84
mf
mf - p
332
sff
ff
marcatiss.
336
poco meno f
molto
𝅗𝅥 = 56
fff
p calm
340
pp
p espr.
344
ppp
ppp calm
349
355
(p)
359

✲ m. 387 - 394 : accel + rit. apply only to Trumpet 2, not to Trombone 1.

Trombone 2

ELLIOTT CARTER

BRASS QUINTET

(1974)

1993 edition

Associated Music Publishers, Inc.

DISTRIBUTED BY
HAL•LEONARD®
7777 W. BLUEMOUND RD. P.O. BOX 13819 MILWAUKEE, WI 53213

Trombone 2

For the American Brass Quintet

BRASS QUINTET

ELLIOTT CARTER
(1974)

All "rips" should sound as many notes as possible.

Dynamics: The dynamic markings are "absolute" - that is, forte in one part should sound as loud as the forte of the other players.

Trombone 2

40
Hn.
as fast as possible)
42
(♩ = 90 or faster)
44
46
(ritardando
♩ = 45)
meno f
48
Tbn.1
♩. = 60
pp calm
52
f angry
58
Tpt.1
Hn.
Tpt.1
f angry
(♩ = 90)
64
Tpt.2
f angry
Tbn.1
meno
Tpt.1

Trombone 2

71
♩ = 108
Tpt.1
Tpt.2
pp calm
5
79
4
4
(♪. = 144)
3
Tpt.2
♩ =72
93 Tpt.2
p majestic
p
pp
96
♩. = 48
p secco
sim.
mp
99
♩ = 96
9
Hn.
Tpt.1
mf
102
7
f
105
110
♪. = 96
mp - p

Trombone 2

Trombone 2

149
Tpt.2
Hn.
151
Tbn.1
"rip"
gliss.
extravagant
153
marc.
155
157
159
Tbn.1
162
cresc. poco a poco
164
"rip"

Trombone 2

166
gliss.
"rip"
f - mf
f > p < mf
"rip"
f
ff
168
ff
ff molto espr.
legato
(ff)
f "rip"
(as before)
172
meno f
ff
f
mf
f > mf
175
♪ = ♪ ♩. = 64
mf
mf
p
mf - p
mp > p
179
pp
f
mf
angry
f
sff - p
pp
p < mf
(vigorous)
184
p
pp
p
espr.
(♩ = 96)
pp
mf
dramatic
189
mf - p
mf
p
f
f
ff
angry
sf - mf
ff
mf
193
Tpt.2
Tb.1
Hn.
Tpt.1
(♪. = 128)
Trp.1
f
mf
p
mf
p
pp
(pp)
197
Tpt.2
Hn.
mf
p
pp
ppp
mf

Trombone 2

230
♩ = 100
ff - f
ff - mf
ff
ff - mf p
234
string. rit. a tempo
2
2
6
mf
247 Hn. Solo
f (non dim.)
angry
251
♩ = 60
p pp
f
Tbn. 1
257
♪. = 96
261
(♩ = 72, ♪. = 96)
Tpt. 1
264 Tbn. 1
Tpt. 1
Tpt. 2
mf
p
(>)
mp
267 Tbn. 1
mp
270
♩. = 72
(𝅗𝅥 = 54, ♩ = 108)
4
3
rubato
a tempo

Trombone 2

281
(♩ =108)
Tpt.1
♩ = 90
284
Tpt.1
ff angry
Tbn.1
(♩. = 60)
287
Tb.1
Hn.
Tpt.2
Tpt.1
𝅗𝅥 = 60, ♩ =120
Hn.
Tbn.1
291
Hn.
Tb.1
295
Hn.
Tb.1
299
[optional]
(hurry slightly - - - - a tempo)
302
pp sub.
Hn.
Tb.1
305
Hn.
[optional]
(hurry slightly - - - - a tempo)
Tb.1

Trombone 2

308
Tb.1
312
Tpt.1
315
= 60 accel.
319
= 126
dramatic
angry
324
(♩. = 84)
= 84
dramatic
329
marcatiss.
335
poco meno
molto
= 56
338
pp calm
341
dramatic
pp calm
p espr.

Trombone 2

345
(𝅗𝅥 = 56)
Tbn.1
Tpt.1
351
357
362
367
372
377
383
(𝅗𝅥 = 56)
388
𝅗𝅥 = 70
5
Tpt.2
𝅗𝅥 = 40 (♩ =80)
Tb.1
396
ff marc. dramatic
"rip"
398

Horn in F

ELLIOTT CARTER

BRASS QUINTET

(1974)

1993 edition

Associated Music Publishers, Inc.

DISTRIBUTED BY
HAL•LEONARD®
7777 W. BLUEMOUND RD. P.O. BOX 13819 MILWAUKEE, WI 53213

F Horn

For the American Brass Quintet

BRASS QUINTET

ELLIOTT CARTER
(1974)

* The horn is notated one fifth above actual sound, regardless of clef.

The dynamic markings throughout are "absolute" - that is, forte in the horn part should sound as loud as the forte of the other players, etc.

30
(𝅗𝅥 = 48)
Tbn.2
vigorous
34
38
(string. [optional] - - - as fast as possible)
41
(♩ = 90 or faster)
44
(ritardando
47
𝅗𝅥 = 45)
Tbn.1
(♩. = 60)
angry
(cresc.)

F Horn

* For measures 72-95 and 194-210, the horn player should use a mute that matches as nearly as possible the nasal quality of that of the second trumpet.

81
Tpt.2
84
87 (♪. =144)
90
♩ = 72
93
95

F Horn

97
♩. = 48
Tpt.2
senza sord.
mf espr.
majestic
secco
100
♩ = 96
Tpt.2
Tpt.1
(4)
103
meno f
(pp)
107
111
♪ = 96
115
(♩ = 72)
mf humorous

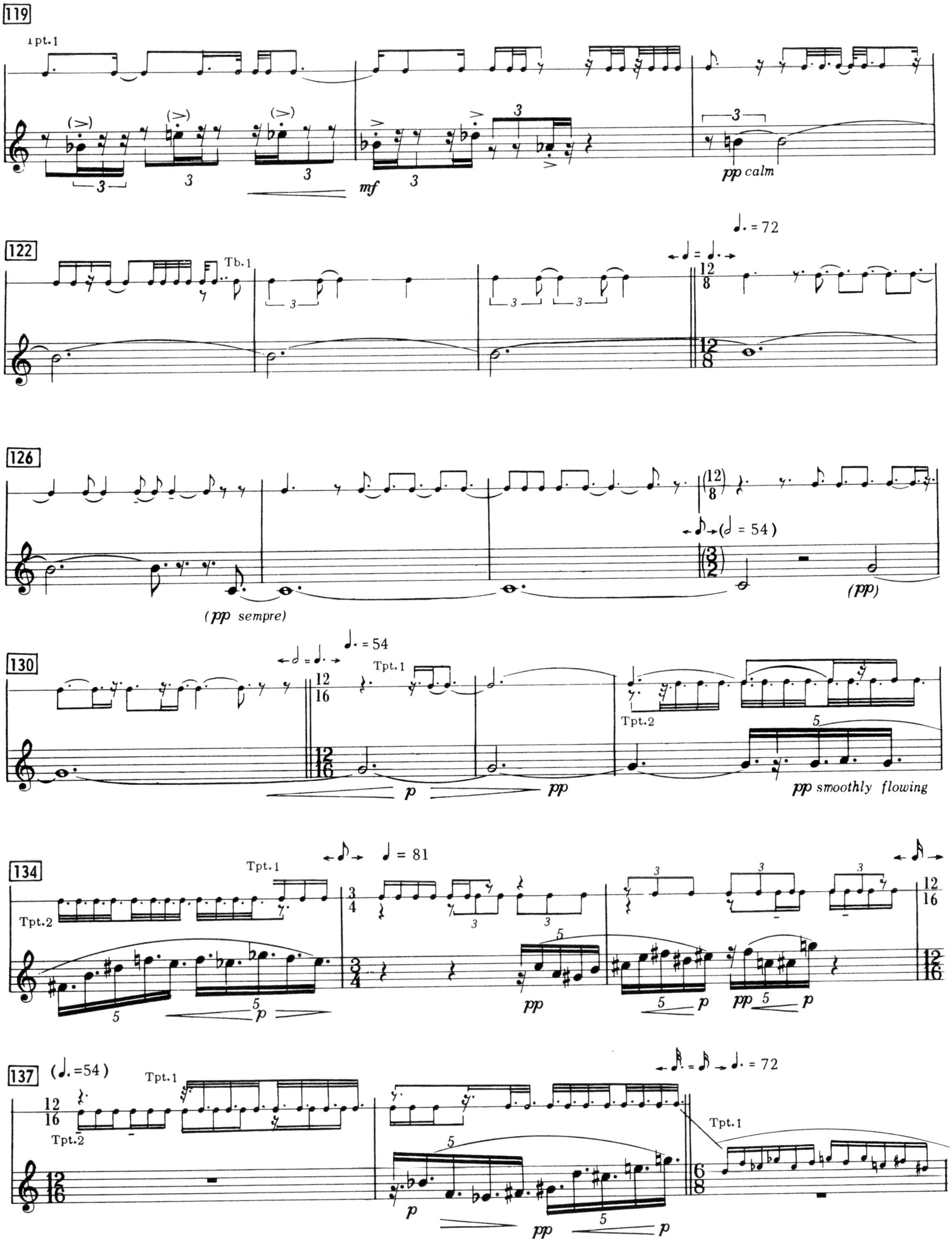
119
Tpt.1
(>)
mf
pp calm
122
Tb.1
♩. = 72
126
(pp sempre)
(♩ = 54)
(pp)
130
♩. = 54
Tpt.1
Tpt.2
p
pp
pp smoothly flowing
134
♩ = 81
p
pp
137
(♩. =54)
♩. = 72

F Horn

154
Tpt.1
Tpt.2
mp
mf
f
mp-p
p
156
mp
mf
158
♩ = 84
pp
(♪. =112)
♩=112
163
Tbn.1
169
majestic
mp
f-mf
173
177
♩. = 64
mf-p
mp-p
180
fp
angry
sff-p
(lightly)

186
(♩=96)
mf
f
menacing
mf
dramatic
f
190
mf
p
f
f
ff
sf-mf
angry
ff
mf
Tpt. 2
♪=128
Tbn. 1
Tbn. 2
193
con sord.
f
f
p humorous
mf
p
pp
(pp)
197
Tpt. 2
Tbn. 1
mf
p
pp
ppp
mf
200
♪=106.7 (♩.=53.3)
mp
p
pp
p
mf
p
pp
accomp.
202
♩=80
Horn: alternate notation
pp
p
pp
pp
p
pp

204
(Hn. alternate notation)
Tpt. 2
206
208
210
7

F Horn

⊕ "Echo tone": This special effect is produced by fingering the pitch a semi tone higher than the written note and flatting it by cupping the hand in the bell, sometimes called 'half stopping'. It is described in Gunther Schuller's Horn Technique, Oxford University Press and in Domenico Ceccarossi's Le Possibilità Coloristiche del Corno (Rome, 1949) It is indicated by the sign: ⊕

* Trill on one note : fingerings for the G and F double-sharp should be used that produce the same pitch but with two different colorations.

F Horn

270
♩. = 72
Rubato
a tempo
281
Tpt. 1
284
♩ = 90
Tbn. 1
ff angry
287
Tbn. 2
290
f sub.
ff sub.
294
Tb. 1
Tb. 2
298
Tbn. 2
[optional]
(hurry slightly
a tempo)
302
Tbn. 1
[optional]
(hurry slightly
a tempo

306
Tb. 2
Tbn. 1
Tbn. 2
mf
f
p
310
ff-f
314
Tpt. 1
sfz
ff
sff
fff
sfff
accel.
♩ = 60
319
♩ =126
gliss. 13
f-mf
dramatic
322
angry
♩. = 84
327
♩ = 84
mp
fp
331
marcatiss.
335
poco meno f
molto
𝅗𝅥 = 56
338
pp
calm
342
p espr.
ppp

F Horn

348
(𝅗𝅥 = 56)
pp
pp
353
pp
mp
358
p
pp
p
pp
p
mf
p
mp
363
ppp
pp
p
pp
p
mp
368
p
mp
mf
p
p
pp
p
p
372
p
mf
f
mf
mf
mp
377
mf
p
mf
f
sff
mf
382
mp
p
pp
p
pp
pp
5
388
𝅗𝅥 = 70
4
Tpt. 2
(poco rit.)
7
7
𝅗𝅥 = 40 (♩=80)
3
396
3
gliss.
ff
6
dramatic
3
marc.
3
3
mf
398
+
gliss.
(+)
ff
(♭)
mf
f
fff